*Stacia -
Snoocn to the
nectcn!
B*

THE NEW BIZARRO AUTHOR SERIES
PRESENTS

I'M NOT EVEN SUPPOSED TO BE HERE TODAY

BRIAN ASMAN

ERASERHEAD PRESS
PORTLAND, OREGON

ERASERHEAD PRESS
P.O. BOX 10065
PORTLAND, OR 97296

www.eraserheadpress.com
facebook/eraserheadpress

ISBN: 978-1-62105-290-6

Printed in the USA.

AUTHOR'S NOTE

As you've probably inferred from the cover of this book, I happen to be a fan of Kevin Smith.

I'm sure there are plenty of people with a more encyclopedic knowledge of the View Askewniverse, but how many of those jerks have written a novella about K.S.? When you've got a stroking-out homeless person accidentally chanting an ancient demon-summoning spell at a convenience store, well, how can you not reference *Clerks*? And once you've opened the portal to that particular circle of the mid-'90s, there's no telling what other references might come through. *Mallrats? Chasing Amy? Dogma?*

Anything but *Yoga Hosers,* clearly.

Although I'd like to think this novella is more of a heartfelt nod to a guy who's spent the last year turning his life around in some pretty amazing ways, and not a *Family Guy*-esque pastiche of references. Kevin Smith's oeuvre is clearly an inspiration, but let's get real, I stole the plot from *Ghostbusters.* Hey, if *Suicide Squad* can do it so can I.

I came to Kevin Smith's work through a circuitous but nevertheless appropriate path. Sometime in the late '90s, I was wandering the racks of my local comic book store when I came across *Clerks: The Comic Book*. Jim Mahfood's graffiti-inspired art style grabbed me right away. I flipped open the comic and it seemed up my alley—a couple slackers hanging out at a convenience store and bullshitting about *Star Wars* while a different pair of slackers sling drugs on the sidewalk outside. Sixteen-year-old me was harboring a set of astonishingly-low aspirations and the world of View Askew seemed an idealized version of that—a gritty sort of paradise where happiness is a forty, a dub sack, and denying children the latest *Happy Scrappy Hero Pups* flick. At the time I was pushing a mop bucket at a rec center and angling for a promotion to the front desk. Working at a fucking video store seemed a dream come true, and if someone's selling pot out front? Even better.

That comic was my gateway drug. I rented the movie version, from a clerk who wasn't nearly as cool or snarky as Randall (although let's get real, sixteen-year-old me would have been scared shitless to rent from a guy like that), and loved the hell out of it. When I got my wisdom teeth out *Mallrats* got me through it, and before I knew it I was watching *Dogma* in theaters. *Jay and Silent Bob Strike Back* presciently nailed the ways I wish I could deal with Internet rage—flying around the country beating the shit out of trolls sounds way more empowering than deleting the Facebook app from my phone yet again.

My protagonist, Scot Kring, thinks *Clerks 2* is a "worthy sequel," and in case you're wondering I'm in full-throated agreement. Maybe the donkey show stuff is a little much, but the sequel captures many of the things I loved about the first one—the brotherly dynamic between Dante and Randall, the hell that is customer service, the incredible one-liners ("One semester we took criminology for God's sake! Criminology! Who the fuck were we studying to be, Batman?"). The *Lord of the Rings* rant is every bit as legendary as the original's *Star Wars* rant. And in the final scenes, Smith brings it home with Randall and Dante out of Mooby's purgatory and back where they belong.

Kevin Smith has made some flicks I truly love and to which I often return. But even more than what he's done, I'll always respect the way Kevin Smith has done it. He's an artist with an utterly unique vision he was hell-bent on sharing with the world, and he did it on his own terms. He had a movie he wanted to make and he made it.

I've always thought the highest compliment anyone can give an artist is that they've made something no one else could—drawing a picture that could only come from their hand or turning a phrase that could only have come from their pen. And that's who Kevin Smith is. Love him or hate him, you can't watch a Kevin Smith film without noticing the intrinsic *Kevin-Smithness* of it.

Kevin Smith makes movies no one else could have made. And that's reason enough to celebrate his work.

Brian Asman
San Diego, CA October 2018

The second time Scot Kring fought a demon straight out of the pits of hell was in a fucking convenience store parking lot.

Pulling his 2004 Chevy S10 into the Fasmart off Garnet, Scot tapped the steering wheel in time to an Alkaline Trio song about girlfriends and pocket knives blasting through Bose speakers Scot had installed himself. He spent his days doing that very thing at SavMore Electronics, taking dashes apart, popping in the latest Bluetooth-equipped head units with removable faceplates, dropping subwoofers into the trunks of Japanese imports. It was an okay gig, as jobs went. He liked working with his hands, and every time he screwed someone's dash back in he felt like he'd actually accomplished something. Not like Carl's Jr. Nothing against them, he just hated hot grease spraying his forearms.

SavMore Electronics offered a mostly grease-free environment, and his boss let him skip out to go surf for an hour or two if they weren't busy. Jenny liked to surf too, and he'd cover for her sometimes, but they'd never paddled out together.

The Fasmart parking lot was mostly empty, except for a dark SUV in front of the defunct nail salon it shared a strip mall with, so Scot pulled right up to one of the spaces in front of the double doors. A balding guy with a wreath of long grey hair and an unkempt beard, wearing a dirty tie-dye tank top, hung around the front entrance.

"Fuckin' panhandlers," Scot muttered to himself, casting a glance through the back window at his 9'8" Walden sticking out of the truck bed, tied down with candy-colored bungee cords. He figured it'd be okay for a minute—he was just running in to get a quick Slushpuppy, and then it was back to work. He'd already been gone a little bit longer than usual, but the waves were that good. Besides, hardly anybody was out at Old Man's, except for a couple actual old men, and Scot had no problem out-paddling anyone who looked so swollen in their wetsuit a simple flick of the finger might cause them to burst. He'd ruled the break that day, taking his pick of waves. Carving long, lazy lines with his longboard. Softly walking across the waxy surface and sticking his toes off the edge, while the sun, out uncharacteristically early for the typically gloomy San Diego June, beat down fiercely. The sunburn on the back of his neck, the salt crystals glued to his skin, even the rash forming on his sparsely-furred chest, since he'd run out the door of his apartment that morning in such a hurry he'd forgotten his rashguard, all were battle scars, oceanic Purple Hearts. As he opened the car door he caught a glimpse of himself in the rearview, and realized he was grinning like a loon.

The stoke was very fucking real.

Scot lowered a bare foot down to the asphalt, quickly retracting it with a yelp like he'd just stepped in lava. The air above its surface wavered with the heat, making the ground look like he was viewing it through a funhouse mirror. His feet were heavily calloused from spending so much time barefoot, but the parking lot was so hot even his calluses couldn't protect him. He wondered how hot it would have to get before the white lines demarcating the parking slots started to melt, running in rivulets across the asphalt like pale boiling blood.

He shivered, despite the heat—*pale boiling blood.* Not exactly an image he'd seen before, but one he could imagine seeing. Not the most pleasant of thoughts, especially after a couple hours spent raging wave after wave.

Scot grabbed his Sanuks off the passenger seat and threw them to the ground, stepping directly into them. He walked around the front of his truck, headed for the double glass doors that led into the air-conditioned paradise that was Fasmart. The windows were covered in advertisements—cigarettes and sports drinks, mostly. An odd combination, but Scot figured most of the people who drank those electrolyte-replacement drinks weren't actually athletes, just regular people with wicked hangovers. He'd been there, on occasion. Nothing like a lemon-lime Gatorade to wash away the sins of the night before.

Combined with a bacon breakfast burrito from Ron Gilberto's, obviously.

As he reached for the front door, the homeless guy cleared his throat and said, "Hey, man, you got any change?"

Scot paused. The guy actually smelled like patchouli, which wasn't much of an improvement from the standard-issue piss and B.O bouquet favored by the worst-off of his brethren. The man pulled a ratty bandana out of the pocket of his jeans and mopped his brow. To say he was sweating profusely seemed reductive. It looked like every drop of moisture in the man's body was fleeing for greener pastures.

"I don't have any cash," Scot said, even though he had a couple twenties crumpled in the pocket of his boardshorts. "But I'll buy you a sandwich or something."

"No thanks, man," the homeless guy said, shaking his beard back and forth. "I'm on a raw food diet."

You should be on a see-food diet, Scot thought, but didn't say anything. This was California, after all. Vegan street people were par for the course. He pulled open the door with a jangle. "Have a good one."

"Can you get me a Gatorade, then? It's hotter'n blazes out here. I feel like I'm about to have a stroke."

Scot nodded. "Sure. What flavor do you want?"

The homeless guy scratched his chin for a second. "I get to pick?"

"Yeah, I don't see why not."

"Hmm, hmm, hmm," the homeless guy said, fiddling with the hem of his tank top. "Something blue, I guess. I've always liked drinking blue things."

"Yeah, okay."

"Thanks man, you're a real lifesaver," the homeless guy said to his back as Scot turned and finally walked through the doorway into the deliciously cool convenience store. He gave a nod to the lady behind the counter and headed towards the Slushpuppy machine in the back. The top of the machine was decorated with the usual outdated advertisements the Fasmart always had for some reason— this one was a cardboard cutout of The Toxic Avenger from his bizarre '90s kids cartoon. Where they'd even gotten the thing, Scot had no idea. The Fasmart was like a weird time capsule. They somehow still sold Nestle Alpine White bars, although Scot would never, ever risk biting into one.

For his money, nothing beat what he called the 'Murica Slushpuppy after a killer surf sesh. Taking a clear sixty-four ounce cup out of the holder, he filled the bottom third with cherry, the middle with pina colada, and the top with blue raspberry. Snapping a lid on the top and poking a straw through, he regarded the upper layer and mused that maybe he did have something in common with the transient melting in the parking lot.

Speaking of, Scot went to the cooler and pulled out a Cool Blue Gatorade and then, noticing the "Two for Three Bucks" sign, grabbed a Lemon-Lime for himself. He took a brief look around the store, wondering if he needed anything else. His eyes lingered on the surf magazines in the newstand rack—if it was slow when he got back to work, he might want something to read. It *was* a Tuesday, after all. But those magazines were so expensive these days. Scot figured he'd just watch some videos on his phone or something.

Said phone buzzed, and he juggled his pending purchases deftly so he could pull it out with one hand. Jenny.

"Yo," he said. "I'm sorry, I know I'm late, but the waves—"

"It's cool," Jenny said quickly, her voice almost a squeal. "Just get back here as soon as you can. You will *never* believe who's buying a Paradigm Sub 1 for his Escalade."

One of the Gatorades started sliding out of his hand, but Scot quickly adjusted, pinning the cool bottle to his chest. "I dunno, who?"

"Kevin...fucking...Smith!" Jenny said, exploding into a tittering bout of laughter. "You *have* to get back here, Scot."

"Holy shit," Scot muttered. He *loved* Kevin Smith's movies. *Dogma* was probably his favorite, although depending on who asked he'd rep the original *Clerks*. And he was in the minority of people who actually thought *Clerks 2* was a worthy sequel. Maybe it was just his Jersey boy bias. He'd grown up surfing LBI before cutting west for California. For his money, Kevin Smith's movies were some of the greatest of all time. Smith's dialogue never failed to make him laugh. Although he'd only made it partway through *Zack and Miri Make a Porno*, always falling asleep right around the time Justin Long started talking about guys dropping their balls into his mouth.

"Don't you mean *snootch to the nootch?*" Jenny said. "Look, we're all out of Paradigm Sub 1s, we're having one brought over from the Temecula store, so you've got a little time. Gary set him up with an Xbox over in the television department and diverted the loss prevention people to keep all the customers away. Anyway, just get back here, and *you can install Kevin Smith's motherfucking subwoofer.*"

Scot almost dropped his phone. He was in shock.

"No fucking way," he said quietly. "No fucking way. This is amazing."

"So why are you still talking to me?" Jenny said. "Get your butt back here. Um, how were the waves by the way?"

"Lotta fun ones out there," Scot said in a daze. This was shaping up to be the best day of his life. "Hey, I'm at Fasmart, I'll just wrap up here and get on back."

"Ooh, you're at Fasmart? Get me a banana Slushpuppy?"

"Banana?" Scot recoiled at the thought. "Ugh."

"Pssh, says the guy who likes Pina Colada."

"*Only* as part of a 'Murica Slushpuppy," Scot said indignantly. "Not like I'd ever get one of those on its own." His Slushpuppy was melting, beads of condensation running down his wrist. Craning his neck, he took a big slurp from the straw, savoring the three combined flavors that tasted like every great day he'd ever had. Immediate refreshment.

"Whatever, dude, just get me a banana. Or I'll let Jordy install Kevin Smith's subwoofer."

"Jordy? Are you fucking kidding me? That son of a—"

"Calm down," Jenny said, laughing. "I'll wait for you. But I'm serious about that banana Slushpuppy."

"It's gonna be all melted by the time I get back."

"I like them melted."

Scot shivered at the thought. "You got it." He hung up and slid the phone back in his pocket, then rejuggled his purchases and walked back to the Slushpuppy machine. He briefly looked over the various cup sizes, trying to decide what Jenny would want, before pulling out another 64-ouncer. He'd rather give her too much than leave her wanting more. Although how anyone could actually want a banana Slushpuppy, he'd never know. Banana Slushpuppies tasted like ball sweat and broken dreams.

The front door jingled, and Scot turned his head to see a couple skater kids walking in, a boy and a girl. They made their way to the refrigerated shelves in the back of the store and started perusing the Pizza Pouches, occasionally play-punching or shoving each other.

Just as he was snapping the lid on Jenny's Slushpuppy, he heard a banging on the front window and almost splattered faux-banana gunk all over his Sanuks. The homeless guy was pressed up against the glass, right next to a Yoohoo ad, mouthing something at Scot. He stuck out his tongue, pantomiming heavy panting before pretending to take a drink out of an invisible container.

The fuck's wrong with this guy, Scot thought. *Entitled assclown.* Back in Jersey, the bums would *never* tell a guy to hurry up if he'd already agreed to buy them something. Here, though, Scot wasn't terribly surprised. He thought about taking the Gatorade back to the cooler, but he figured it *was* pretty hot outside. Even if the guy was kind of a dick, Scot could still do something nice for him. And with all the good things coming Scot's way, first the killer session and now Kevin fucking Smith's Escalade job, he might as well earn himself some good karma.

Scot quickly topped off his own Slushpuppy, the drink having already reached the point in its deliquescence where the layered flavors were hopelessly commingled, and then hurried to the counter. The clerk was idly watching the hot dogs turning on the grill and picking at something under one of her nails.

"Hi," Scot said with a smile, pushing his purchases across the counter. The clerk ignored him at first, but he forced himself to stand there patiently until the overcooked bags of pig rectums lost their appeal and she turned to him. *Karma.*

"This all?" she asked with a slight southern drawl.

"Yep," Scot said, "That's it."

The clerk rung him up, lacquered nails moving ponderously across the keys of the cash register. Scot drummed his fingers on the counter, inadvertently tapping out the rhythm to the Alkaline Trio song he'd been listening to when he pulled into the parking lot, still stuck in his head. Finally she gave him the total, and he paid with a credit card. Scooping up his purchases, the clerk tried to hand him a receipt, but he waved her off with his chin.

"No thanks," Scot said.

The expressionless clerk tossed the receipt in his direction. It floated down to the counter. Scot looked at the receipt, then at the clerk, then the receipt again.

The homeless guy banged on the window.

Scot felt like he *had* to take the receipt, like he was an asshole if he didn't, and today of all days, he had to be a nice guy. Otherwise, maybe he'd get back to SavMore just in time to see an Escalade with a brand new Paradigm Sub 1 in the cargo bay installed by goddamn *Jordy* pull away.

"Uh, I don't think I need a receipt," Scot tried again. The banging on the window got louder, but the clerk didn't seem to notice. Her eyes flicked back to the hot dogs. Juices beaded on their surfaces like sweat, and one had already burst open at the ends. Clearly beyond done.

The receipt sat there on the counter like a turd in a punchbowl. The homeless guy kept banging on the window. And in his arms, Scot's two Slushpuppies kept melting.

"I guess I'll just take it," Scot said, pressing his four drinks to his chest, reaching down with one hand to snag the receipt by its edge. He looked around for a trashcan, but the closest one was back by the Slushpuppy machine, right under Toxie's green grinning visage, so he just shoved it down in his pocket. "Have a nice day." The clerk didn't respond.

As he turned for the door, he realized the banging had stopped. The homeless guy wasn't pressed up against the glass anymore. Scot shot a glance at the back of his truck, hoping the guy hadn't decided to abscond with his stick. The red and white tail still stuck out the back.

Maybe he got bored, Scot thought. *Oh well, nothing wrong with having* two *Gatorades.*

At the door Scot laughed as he always did at the height chart, a criminal version of the hash marks his mother had put on the inside of the basement door every couple months from the time he could keep his wobbly little toddler legs under him until summer break his freshman year of college. He pushed backwards through the door, leaving behind the cool conditioned air of the Fasmart, and entered the boiling late morning heat.

Tripping over a pair of dirty sneakers.

Scot did a little dance but managed not to eat it.

The homeless guy laid in front of the door, eyes rolled back in his skull, head lolled to the side, his whole body spasming. The man's tongue flopped obscenely between his lips while thick spittle ran down the sides of his mouth. Brown-and-yellow mucus oozed from both nostrils. A noise emanated from his mouth, or rather a *series* of noises. Inhuman gibberish, mostly.

"Caradara habba nanna gluckaluckhi," the homeless guy spat as he shook.

"Oh shit!" Scot cried out, dropping the Gatorades which hit the ground and rolled off the curb, lodging against the concrete parking block. He nearly dropped the Slushpuppies too, but had the presence of mind to turn and set them down by the window, away from the homeless guy's flailing feet.

"Are you alright?" Scot said, immediately realizing how dumb the words sounded coming out of his mouth. Of course the guy wasn't alright, he was having a fucking seizure or something.

Scot yanked the door to the Fasmart open and called to the clerk, "Hey! There's a guy out here, call 911?"

She gaped at him a moment, then turned to pick up the phone. The skater kids dropped their Pizza Pouches to the ground with twin *splats,* pulling phones from their pockets to film whatever was going on outside. Scot shut the door and turned back to the guy. He'd taken a first aid class back in high school. He remembered the CPR part, but that didn't seem like something the guy needed. Plus the guy had a mouthful of thick gurgling spit and brown and broken teeth that Scot wasn't about to get his lips near. He tried to remember what you were supposed to do for a seizure. Something about immobilizing the body?

He just stood there, shaking his head in confusion. Scot shot a look back inside. The clerk was still on the phone, the skater kids still filming the scene for FlickerSnip or Momentamize or whatever. Hopefully the ambulance would get there soon. The fire station was just down the street. He looked around the parking lot, out at the bus stop in front, the sidewalk, to see if he could flag down anyone who might be useful, but he didn't see another soul. He was alone in the parking lot with the homeless guy and his rapidly-melting Slushpuppies and the heat wavering above the asphalt.

"Homina gomina glomina gliddy gloo!"

Scot stuck his head back inside the door, cool air conditioning washing over his sunburnt forehead. "Tell them to hurry! I don't know what to do!"

The homeless guy rolled over on his stomach, flopping around like a fish out of water. His dirty palms slapped the ground, his head jerking back like it was trying to bend itself over his spine. He inched forward like a seal, until he was directly below the anachronistic payphone that Scot occasionally saw people who looked more or less like the seizing homeless man at his feet use.

The homeless guy lashed out with a hand and caught the cord, ripping the phone from its cradle. The receiver tumbled end-over-end in slow motion until it hit the ground and cracked open, spilling out its intestinal wiring.

"Nibby moo moo skukka rukka hey!"

Not sure what else to do, Scot looked through the window again The clerk was still on the phone.

He wondered if she'd actually called 911 or if she'd just called a friend to chat about the overcooked hot dogs rolling around and around on the grill. Or maybe about the asshole customer who didn't want his receipt. Of course the skater kids could have called an ambulance too, instead of ghoulishly documenting the man's medical emergency. He took a step away from the bum and listened for sirens in the distance. Far, far away, he maybe heard a wail, but it could have just been another bum in the alley screaming about ghost badgers or the Illuminati. Or one of the fucking wild parrots that made PB their home.

Scot was about to pull his own phone out and call 911 when he heard something that made his blood run cold.

"Nibby mum scurlous influp diggium dee ibis!"

Scot froze, his hand hovering right outside the pocket of his board shorts, now even less sure what to do than he had been before. The bum's nonsense sounded familiar. Too familiar, a garbled allusion to the worst night of Scot's life—after a Darrow Chemical Company show, in the back of a shitty broken down club somewhere in northern Jersey. When an idiot, probably concussed from taking too many shots in the pit, read some Latin words he definitely, definitely shouldn't have.

"Shut up!" Scot screamed, but that didn't help. The man rolled over onto his back, his legs and upper body twisting horribly like he was cosplaying as a question mark. Scot locked eyes with him. The man's own rheumy peepers stared back full of fear, giving him a window into the man's mind. Still aware enough to experience what was happening to him, to know he'd lost control.

"Nimibuum storklos ferby dicktum!"

As if possessed himself, Scot jumped on top of the bum, grabbing at his gibbering mouth, trying to force it shut. Unlikely though it was, he knew deep down in his bones that if the man kept spouting nonsense, he was going to spout exactly the *wrong* nonsense, and then they'd all be well and truly fucked.

Just like last time.

The man bucked like a bronco underneath Scot, batting at his face and head with grubby hands. Scot tried to ignore the assault, and the greasy film the man's appendages left in their wake, and focused on shutting the man's mouth. With one hand, he gripped a fistful of beard, while with the other he grabbed the man's nose, leveraging his mouth closed. The man's tongue pushed dryly against Scot's palm, but Scot didn't care. Better to sever the fucking thing than have the man say what Scot knew he was about to say.

"Shut up, shut up, shut up!" Scot hissed in the bum's face, spouting a mantra of his own. He only hoped it was enough.

"Hey, what the hell are you doing? Get off him!"

Scot cocked his head slightly and saw two EMTs running up behind him, one carrying a medical bag. Both pumping their arms furiously, looks of concern on their faces. An ambulance was parked haphazardly behind them, its blue and red lights still flashing. The fire truck must have been running behind, but he could hear more sirens headed their way.

Annoyed at the interruption, Scot said, "I'm just trying to—"

The bum reached up with a filthy finger and poked

Scot right in the eye.

He recoiled, hands instinctively going to his face. Beneath him, the bum shifted, and two hands grabbed him by his t-shirt and tossed him to the side with hysterical strength. Scot landed roughly on his hip, scrambling to get back up.

But before he could, the bum opened his mouth and shouted, "Nimirum circulos inferni dicam de imis tenebris!"

And just like that, the millionth monkey hopped on the millionth typewriter for the millionth time and wrote the opening lines to *A Tale of Two Cities*.

The air around them shifted slightly, first a few degrees cooler, then much, much warmer. The homeless man stopped convulsing and lay still, as if he was suddenly aware of the enormity of what he'd done. Out in the street, a passing car slowed and then bizarrely sped up, skipping in place like a movie missing a few frames. The two EMTs staggered to a halt a few feet away, standing there dumbly, looking around and trying to figure out what the hell was going on.

"Fuck my life," Scot muttered, even as the phone in his pocket start to buzz again. Jenny, probably wondering where he was, and more importantly where her Slushpuppy was.

Unless Scot pulled off a miracle, she wouldn't be getting a Slushpuppy today. And maybe ever again.

A cloud passed in front of the sun and the sky turned black. A deeper, darker black than any moonless night. Not the color of the void, but the color of the absence of the void itself. A color of less than nothing. Antinothing. In response, the sodium floodlights circling the parking lot flipped on, a valiant and mindless attempt to beat back the dark.

Beneath Scot's feet, the ground began to shake.

Scot grabbed on to the nearest thing at hand, the now-useless pay phone. He held on for dear life as the concrete beneath his feet bucked and swayed like the surface of the ocean. "Fuck!"

"What's going on?" one of the EMTs shouted, legs staggering underneath him as he tried to regain his balance. His partner had already fallen flat on her face, her rubber-gloved hands grabbing asphalt to try to hang on to the ground in lieu of better options.

"Nothing good!" Scot called back. "Grab on to whatever you can!"

"What is this, an earthquake?" the female EMT shouted from the ground.

"That's part of it," Scot said, as the wind kicked up to hurricane gale force, blowing his sunbleached hair back. Despite the wind, the air was disgustingly hot, and sweat ran from his forehead, down the back of his neck, from his armpits. A few feet away, his truck creaked on its springs.

The male EMT launched himself through the air and slammed into the glass windows of the Fasmart, snatching at the other side of the payphone enclosure. He hauled himself in and looked at Scot. "This ain't no damn earthquake, is it?"

"Not exactly." Scot didn't even bother asking why the EMT thought he was an authority on what was going on. He figured he just had that look, the look of someone who's seen all this before.

The EMT shot a glance at his partner, who'd been

blown into the side of Scot's truck. She desperately clutched the side view mirror, even as the wind threatened to lift her feet off the ground and send her flying.

"Darla! Come here!" He held out a hand to her, even though she was too far away to grasp it.

Darla gritted her teeth, just trying to hold on. The wind ripped her hair tie out and sent her long brown curls fanning out behind her. The side view mirror started to wobble under her grip.

Scot shot a look down at the homeless guy. He lay on the ground, undisturbed by the chaos around them, a peaceful and serene look on his face, his eyes half-closed.

Scot did a double-take. The bum wasn't lying *on* the ground. He was lying above it. His body hovered barely an inch off the concrete strip in front of the Fasmart.

"Uh, what's that guy doing?" the EMT said, staring at the bum with a shocked expression on his face.

"Don't worry about him," Scot said. "Worry about—"

The wind suddenly kicked up, and metal groaned as both the ambulance and Scot's truck moved a couple inches.

"Uh oh," Scot said.

But that wasn't the worst of it. The roiling, wavering heat that previously lingered above the asphalt had changed. The air over the asphalt wasn't boiling anymore— the asphalt *itself* was. Bubbles formed on the surface of the blacktop, hissing and popping furiously. The black surface devolved into tar right before Scot's eyes.

Darla tried desperately to hold onto his side view mirror, which had now buckled and folded in. Smoking hot sludge stuck to her boots. "Jesus, what the hell is this?" she screamed, eyes wide with fear, stomping her feet but only succeeding in splashing boiling pitch about. Her movements slowed and her boots sunk down into the tar.

"Hold on to my hand," Scot told the male EMT, who gaped at him a second before grabbing Scot's left forearm with both hands. Scot leaned into the wind, which pushed his eyebrows up in a forced look of surprise, and reached his right arm out to Darla. "Grab on!" he yelled, fingers brushing across the back of the mirror she was holding.

Darla just stared at his hand, her mouth moving wordlessly. Spittle ran freely from the corners. She tried to pick up a foot, but the melting tar surface of the parking lot stuck to her boots, rooting her in place.

"I think I'm stuck."

"Seriously, take my hand!" Scot yelled again.

Slowly, Darla reached out a tentative hand to Scot, her appendage shaking like a wet puppy, still holding on to the side view mirror with the other. Not that she needed to, not anymore—the parking lot itself now held her firm against the wind.

"Closer, closer," Scot said, nodding vigorously, trying to encourage her. "You can do it, uh, Darla."

Darla's hand stretched closer. Just as their fingertips grazed each other, a bolt of red lightning rent the black sky, slashing down from on high to strike the middle of the parking lot, followed closely by a massive thunderclap that threatened to burst Scot's eardrums. Boiling hot asphalt splattered everywhere, some landing on the bum, who took it in stride.

Some landing on Darla, who did not.

She screamed, jerking away from Scot's outstretched

hand, divots of blistering tar showering the back of her head. She let go of the side view mirror, both hands grabbing at her hair, batting at the sticky, smoking patches on the back of her head. The acrid scent of burnt hair filled Scot's nostrils, the unpleasant tang choking him. And underneath it all, the rotten egg stench of sulfur. Scot's stomach churned, not so much from the smell itself, but what it signified.

Time for the main event.

More lightning lit up the sky like electric spider webs crackling in the heavens. The ground shook and spasmed like the homeless guy's body had moments before, sending Darla keeling over backwards. She tried to keep herself upright, hands abandoning the still-burning wounds in the back of her head to snatch uselessly at the quavering air around her, but momentum had her.

As did the smoking sludge that gripped her boots.

Darla finally lost her balance and fell to the ground, but her feet stuck fast, her legs folding awkwardly over as she landed screaming in boiling asphalt. Superheated tar stuck to her arms and face like napalm. Darla's upper body flopped and rolled in counterproductive agony, her thrashing only succeeding in spreading more sweltering asphalt over every inch of her skin.

"Darla!" the EMT screamed and lunged for her, but Scot pushed him back.

"She's gone," Scot snarled. "Nothing you can do for her."

"But—"

"Dude, look at that shit." Scot pointed at the parking lot, which now looked like a vat of boiling oil waiting malevolently on some parapet until the unfortunate attackers were just within range of the castle walls. The white paint that previously marked the parking spots flowed like rivers to the center of the lot, swirling and coalescing into a shape. One very, very familiar to Scot, and anyone who'd ever shopped at a Hot Topic.

A five-pointed star, of course.

Upside down.

"What the hell," the EMT said, jaw hanging open. "Is that what I think it is?"

"Yeah," Scot said. "We need to get inside. Now. See if we can fortify the place." He glanced at the glass doors, which mercifully hadn't been shattered by flying debris or red lightning. The clerk still stood behind the counter, but now the receiver dangled limply from her hand. The two skaters were still recording everything with their phones. *Fucking vultures,* Scot thought. Not that anything they could think to do on their own would help—all things considered they were probably better off staying out of his way.

"What about—"

Scot wanted to slap the EMT across the face, but settled for grabbing him by the lapels and shaking him like a crying infant instead. "She's dead, do you hear me? Leave her."

Tears streaked from the EMT's eyes as he stood there staring at his partner. Darla had stopped screaming. And moving. Her body was nearly unrecognizable, covered as it was in boiling pitch. It reminded Scot of Pompeii—legions of people, all swaddled in dried lava.

He glanced down at the homeless guy, who still

hovered a couple inches off the ground, smiling widely, serenely. Occasionally he nodded his head, and his smile stretched ever wider, threatening to split his face apart. Something was whispering to him from the other side. Speaking in saccharine tongues, telling him things he'd never known he wanted to hear. Scot had seen that look on another face, years before. At the time, he hadn't known what was going on. What it signified. Now that he did, the sight turned his stomach. He wanted to stomp the bum's head in. Splatter that smile all over the concrete strip in front of the Fasmart, paint over the window ads for Camel Lights with his fucking blood.

But self-preservation won out. He *wanted* to stomp the bum's head in. He *needed* to get inside.

"Let's go!" he yelled at the EMT once more.

The pentagram in the middle of the parking lot ascended slowly, expanding from two dimensions to three to more as it spun like a turbine. But the man could only stare dumbly at the remains of his partner.

Scot looked from the EMT to poor dead Darla, to the pentagram and back again. "Fuck it," he said, and as soon as he felt a slight lull in the wind he jumped towards the glass double doors leading into the Fasmart. He caught one handle and ripped the door open, the hinges wobbling queasily. The wind caught the edge of the door and tried to wrench it from his grasp, but he held tight, carefully sliding into the convenience store and shutting the door behind him. Glass wasn't much protection against what they were up against. None at all, in fact. But it made him feel better, and it deadened some of the sounds and smells from outside.

That was no small thing.

"Dude, what the fuck is going on out there?" the boy skater asked.

Scot turned to look at him, wiping sweat away from his brow. "You believe in God?"

The kid shook his purple mohawk back and forth.

"Yeah, me neither." Scot spun on his heel and stalked over to the counter. "You got any salt in this place?" he asked the clerk.

She gaped at him, her eyes straying back towards the hot dogs. All of them had burst now.

"Salt!" Scot shouted in her face.

Still holding the phone, she raised a hand and pointed towards aisle three.

"Salt, salt, salt," Scot repeated to himself, over and over, hurrying towards the indicated aisle. This was apparently the grocery section. His eyes scanned shelf after shelf of canned goods, marshmallow-studded breakfast cereals, dirt-cheap packets of dry noodle products.

Not a bad place to get stuck during an apocalypse, Scot thought to himself. *Way better than the back of a shitty club in New Jersey.*

He quickly located the cylindrical containers of Morton's salt, next to a couple jars of pickles that looked slightly past their expiration date (which, to Scot, was the same day a perfectly good cucumber was consigned to that vile and briny broth in the first place). Scot scooped up as many containers as he could carry, juggling them in his hands. Emerging from the aisle, weighed down with salt, he looked first at the clerk, who seemed nearly as catatonic as the EMT outside, and then to the two skater kids.

"Hey, Tweedledum and Tweedledee, give me a hand here?"

The girl skater put her phone down long enough to cross her arms over her Powell-Peralta tee and give Scot a withering look. "We have names, you know."

"Yeah, I really don't give a shit," Scot said. "If you want to live, give me a hand here."

The girl rolled her eyes and took a step forward. "*Fine.* What do you want us to do?"

Scot held out a container of salt. "Sprinkle this in a line across the front of the store. I'll do the sides and the back. Here, you take one too." He handed another container to Purple Mohawk.

"You want us to make a mess?" Mohawk asked incredulously.

"I want you to help save our lives from *that,*" Scot said, pointing out the windows.

Two multi-colored skater heads turned to follow his finger. Out beyond the Fasmart windows, the parking lot was still bubbling, strings of asphalt leaping through the air like broiling snot. The surviving EMT stood dumbly by the payphone, taking everything in. The pentagram was revolving faster and faster, so quickly Scot wouldn't have been able to tell what it was if he hadn't already seen it forming. Devolving into a Satanic blur, the pentagram descended towards the surface of the parking lot, the asphalt below bubbling up and parting like Moses allegedly did to that sea back in the day to allow the makeshift metaphysical drill access to the earth below. The tip of the pentagram only had to pierce the earth's mantle in order for the thing waiting on the other side to break through.

"Stop gawking and lay down some fucking salt!" he yelled. The skater kids got to work, each starting at opposite ends of the store. Mohawk leaned behind the ATM, shaking his salt container, while the girl skater shoved a pile of plastic-wrapped, pre-cut wood to the side and salted away. Scot headed towards the sides of the store, starting next to the girl's pile. He opened his container and laid down a line of salt, joining his to the one streaking across the front of the store. He didn't bother moving anything, just laid it right down the aisle, past the paltry automotive section, the overstuffed shelves of snack cakes, the astronomically-expensive paper towels and toilet paper for the unfortunate soul who made a mess or had to take a shit after the grocery stores closed. As he passed the Slushpuppy machine, Toxie's radioactive green grin stared back at him. He figured in real life, Toxie would end up just like Darla in the parking lot. No superpowers, just a flash-fried, tumor-ridden chump dying a fucking agonizingly painful death.

Scot finished making his way around the store, laying down a thick layer of salt. The two skater kids had finished the front and stood peering out the windows, their breath fogging the glass, their phones apparently forgotten, for once. Scot joined them at the window, checking the progress in the parking lot.

The pentagram was an indistinguishable blur inches above the earth, while the bum now floated five feet in the air, his ratty broken-heeled shoes level with the male EMT's chin. The EMT himself was still staring blankly out into the parking lot, his back to the store. If Scot could see his eyes, he knew they'd be glazed over, his gaze utterly empty. Like all the sights he'd seen had scooped out the inside of the guy's skull. Some things, people just weren't meant to see. Their minds snapped, like Darla's knees when the viscous asphalt forced them to bend at an impossible angle.

Scot realized he'd put a hand on the shoulder of each of the skater kids without even thinking about it. The three of them stood witness at the window, pulses beating in triple-time.

Watching the end of the world.

The pentagram finally touched down, exploding in a blindingly bright flash that scorched the inside of Scot's retinas. His eyes snapped shut, his hands belatedly covering the wounded orbs. The boy screamed next to him, while the girl uttered a small, choked sob. Behind them, the clerk let out a long, simple "What?"

Scot rubbed his eyes, forcing them open. He saw stars for a moment before the blurred objects in front of him resolved into their normal shapes. A massive hole gaped in the middle of the parking lot. The levitating homeless guy was sucked straight into it feet-first. A single dirty hand clutched ineffectually at nothing before he disappeared entirely below the surface of the earth. Raw materials, for the thing coming across—a scaffolding, on which to build a body fit for the corporeal world.

Scot looked at the skater kids. The boy was sobbing hysterically, while the girl had collapsed to the floor, curling her body into the fetal position. "Whatever you do, clear your heads," he told them. "*Don't* think of anything." He didn't bother relaying his instructions to the clerk—she looked like her last thought had come and gone sometime before she slapped on her orange apron.

"Wha-why?" the girl said, twisting her neck to look up at him with a shell-shocked impression.

"Just trust me," Scot said. "Clear your head. If it helps, just think *nothing* over and over again."

The girl screwed up her face and gave him a curt nod, while the boy just kept wailing. Scot exhaled and forgot about them. Tried to forget about anything. The last time, the demon had played by *Ghostbusters* rules. He wasn't sure how it all worked, but he figured maybe if they didn't think of anything, the demon wouldn't have anything to work with. Wouldn't be able to transform that poor homeless guy's body into an instrument of death and destruction. Might, emphasis on might, say *fuck it* and head right back to hell.

But of course he knew there was no fucking way that was happening.

As Scot stood there, picturing nothing but endless white expanses in his head, featureless dreams of deserts, something started rhythmically tapping against his leg. Not tapping. Vibrating. It took him a minute to realize it was his phone.

Oh shit! he thought. *Kevin Smith!*

Out in the parking lot, a low groan resounded from the hole in the ground, as if in response to his inadvertent thought.

"Oh fuck me, really?" Scot said. He wanted to slap himself.

"What?" asked Skater Girl.

Scot took a deep breath, staring at the hole in the ground, waiting for something to emerge. "I think I just screwed us."

"Wait, what are you talking about, man?" Mohawk asked.

Scot ran a hand through his hair. Realized his phone was still vibrating. He pulled the phone out of his pocket to check the caller ID—just a bunch of sixes. Of course Jenny wouldn't be calling now, a cell phone signal couldn't break through the demonic bubble localized around the Fasmart. They'd fucking gotten him good. Demons were like grandparents, slow to adopt new technology but once they did?

Watch the fuck out.

"Hey, old guy?" Skater Girl said, snapping her fingers in front of his face. "Why'd you say you screwed us?"

Scot took a depth breath, then said, "This is going to sound crazy but that levitating homeless man in the parking lot who just got sucked into a hole in the earth is about to become the vessel for a demon, or demon-like entity, I'm not really sure on the taxonomy, because he was having a stroke and in this really bizarre coincidence accidentally said this Latin phrase that rips open the veil between this world and I guess you could call it Hell."

"Da fuq?" Mohawk asked.

"Yeah, I said the same thing," Scot sighed. "Last time."

"You mean, something like this—" Skater Girl waved a hand at the windows at the front of the store, "—you've *been* through something like this before?"

"A long time ago. Back in New Jersey."

Mohawk and Skater Girl exchanged a look like they'd both caught a whiff of the most rancid fart they'd ever smelled in their lives. "*New Jersey?*"

"So now I'm asking you to trust me. Right now I'm the only one who might be able to get us through this."

"Wait a second though," Skater Girl said. "You just

said you screwed us, now you're the only one who can get us out of this? Which is it, dude? What are you even talking about?"

"You ever see that movie *Ghostbusters?*"

"Like with Melissa McCarthy?" Mohawk said.

"No, not with Melissa McCarthy," Scot said. "The original one. You know, Bill Murray, Ernie Hudson, Dan Ackroyd?"

The two skaters shook their multi-colored heads.

"Harold Ramis?"

"The dad from that old movie *Knocked Up?*"

"Forget about it," Scot said. "Anyway, the demon takes the form of whatever we think of. That's why I told you to clear your minds, see? But I screwed up. My phone started ringing, I think it's my boss, and thinking of Jenny made me think about Kevin Smith. He's at the SavMore right now, waiting for me to install a subwoofer in his Escalade."

"Who?"

"Kevin Smith."

The two skaters stared blankly at him.

"You know, View Askew? *Clerks, Mallrats, Chasing Amy?*"

Nothing.

"*Jay and Silent Bob Strike Back?*"

"Is that for Xbox?"

"Jesus, no it's a movie," Scot huffed. "*Dogma? Cop Out? Zack and Miri Make a Porno?*"

"Oh yeah," Skater Girl said, giggling. "With Seth Rogen! I love him, he's so fucking funny."

"*Knocked Up* was better."

Scot shook his head. He had half a mind to just let the demon have these two.

A violent cry echoed from the hole in the parking lot, shaking the windows. Scot pressed his face against the glass, straining to see what was going on. A shadowy hand emerged from the hole, each finger capped with long curling talons, and dug into the still-steaming asphalt. Another hand followed. And another. Straining against the ground, something began to haul itself out of the hole.

Something big.

"Dude, what *is* that?" Mohawk asked.

Scot eyed the writhing appendages, the impossible angles, the leathery and callused hide that looked like nothing that might be found in nature. "We'll find out in a minute."

The clerk finally dropped the phone in her hand to better stare out the front windows. Her eyes were wide with panic. "I'm not even supposed to be here today."

"Oh Jesus fucking Christ," Scot yelled over his shoulder, his voice cracking. "That's not the only line in the movie."

The clerk mumbled something at him.

"What?"

"Try not to suck any dick on your way to the parking lot!" the clerk shouted, snatching a burst hot dog off the grill and chucking it at Scot's head. It missed by a wide margin and slapped against the window, leaving a thin film of grease as it slid down the glassy surface.

"Stop throwing shit at me. I'm the only one who can get us out of this."

"Didn't you say you're the one who screwed us all?" Skater Girl said petulantly.

"Yeah. Both those things."

"What does that—?"

"Shut up and look!" Scot shouted, pointing out the window.

A black mass sat at the edge of the hole, a tightly wound, throbbing ball of malevolence. Slowly, the ball unfurled, taloned claws slicing at the air, every jerky motion pregnant with hunger and hate. The thing slowly stood up, keeping its head down, stretching all of its otherworldly muscles and tendons, or infernal analogues of such fleshly physiological features—like most transplanted San Diego surfers, Scot wasn't up on his demonic anatomy.

Nothing of the homeless man remained. His flesh had been transmogrified, base material used to build something far stranger. The creature in the parking lot towered over them, maybe ten or twelve feet tall. Its basic shape was that of a human, but stretched and skewed to chthonic proportions. Legs curved back behind it like an elk, ending in hooves, while its three arms, covered in corded muscle, swiped at the air. The strange topography of its flesh, a patchwork of scale and chitin and wiry fur, called to mind a Frankenstein's monster assembled in the trophy room of some laudanum-addled Victorian-era great white hunter. It wore a pair of tattered jorts and a blood-stained hockey jersey.

"Cal—ga—ry Flames," Mohawk sounded out, the four simple syllables stretching the worry lines in his forehead to their utmost limits.

"Oh, very fucking funny," Scot muttered.

The creature lifted its head, revealing a skull shaped like an anvil, covered in dark fur and crowned with a black, backwards baseball cap. A greasy beard clung to its chin. Opening its mouth to let a bloodthirsty roar escape, Scot noted row after row of jagged yellow teeth. The thing was a study in repugnance.

"What the fuck," Skater Girl said. "It's like some kind of *mutant.*"

Scot didn't bother to correct her.

The monster stalked back and forth on unsteady legs, evidently still getting used to its corporeal form, moving like something out of a Harryhausen picture— both goofy and menacing at the same time. At this staccato motion, the EMT finally awoke from his fugue state and screamed.

Scot banged on the window, trying to get his attention. All the guy had to do was run inside and he'd be safe. But the EMT showed no sign he heard the racket Scot was making. Instead he stood frozen, as if boiling tar had leeched onto his own boots and rooted him in place.

The creature awkwardly but quickly made its way across the parking lot, sticky asphalt clinging to its spindly legs, hooves, the ratty hem of its jorts. Unlike Darla, the superheated substance had little effect on the demon. If the stuff burned its scaly hide, it gave no indication whatsoever. It just kept coming, putting one hoof in front of the other, until it stood in front of the screaming EMT.

"Should we like—" Skater Girl started to say, but the creature's actions stilled her tongue.

One of its three claws swiped through the air, slicing down with horrendous strength and separating the EMT's head from his body.

The motion cut off his voice in mid-scream, and then

his head tumbled to the ground, hitting the concrete with a sickening *thwump* and rolling out into the parking lot to rest near the horribly burnt body of Darla.

His body stood in place for a moment, resisting the inevitable, a spurt of blood pumping out of his neck artery and splashing across the creature's face. Then it collapsed, under the weight of gravity and the enormity of what had just happened, the legs folding forward, the body following suit.

Mohawk let out an ear-splitting scream.

"Shut the fuck up," Scot snarled, giving Mohawk a healthy smack.

"Ow!" Mohawk cried, then did what he was told, glowering in Scot's direction as he rubbed his head.

The creature in the parking lot reared back in front of the EMT's corpse and let out a deep belly-laugh, a sickly sound that echoed in Scot's ears and reverberated around inside his skull. A noise that left behind a sussurant echo like a stain, a barely audible voice inside his mind—part infection, part contingency plan. If he listened, really listened, Scot knew he'd be able to hear it making all kinds of promises. Piles of money and harems of women. Waves for days and not a douche in the lineup. Every single desire he'd ever had, made real as soon as he could think it. A cheat code for life.

But he knew it wouldn't be enough, even if he said yes. Every pleasure his limited human mind could imagine would ultimately prove hollow. Pointless. And then he'd blow his own brains out with a gold-plated revolver in front of a room full of naked, coked-up centerfolds.

Just like his buddy Ethan had all those years ago.

Ethan, who'd carried an infernal taint with him out

of the back of that shitty club in northern New Jersey, like a wounded baby bird under his patch-covered jacket.

Ethan, who'd said yes to the voice as the physical manifestation of *that* particular demon had burned.

Ethan, who'd lived just long enough to see the *joie* sucked right out of his *vivre* at the ripe old age of twenty-three.

"Not today!" Scot growled, banging against the glass. "You hear me? *Not today!*"

"Um," Skater Girl began, "do you really think you should—"

The creature lunged forward, smashing into the glass, which of course shattered. The sheer percussive force of the impact threw Scot backwards into a rack of habanero almonds and beef jerky. He hit the floor hard, prepackaged salty treats raining down on his head.

"Shouldn't have done that," Scot muttered, rising unsteadily to his feet. The creature swiped a claw at him through the shattered window but instantly retracted it, howling in pain. The tips of its chitinous claws spewed acrid smoke. Looking down at its wounded appendage, the creature cocked its head, trying to understand what could possibly have hurt it.

"And *stay* out there," Scot said. The circle was working, so there was that. Maybe if SavMore didn't work out he could get a job as a really shitty wizard.

Glass tinkled as Skater Girl got to her feet. "Where's Tanner?" she said, looking around.

Scot couldn't help but laugh, despite the circumstances. "That fucker's name is *Tanner?* Shit, we should just throw him to the demon now. Might give hell boy a little indigestion."

"I'm serious, asshole. Where's—" Her gaze fixed on the Slushpuppy machine, eyes widening, tears leaking from the corners. Scot followed her stare. Mohawk lay beneath the cardboard cutout of the Toxic Avenger, his neck bent at an awkward angle, his eyes open and unfocused while Toxie grinned down from above.

"Shit," Scot said.

Skater Girl sobbed and rushed towards Mohawk's corpse.

Scot let her go, turning instead to face the creature. The circle of salt was keeping it at bay, for the moment. It stalked back and forth in front of the shattered Fasmart windows, occasionally testing the barrier with a claw. Every time it did, it immediately screamed and pulled back a smoking digit, like a child too stupid to stay away from the stove.

Dumb fucker, Scot thought. *Doesn't even realize why it can't get in.* The sight of the demon's pathetic struggle to breach his jury-rigged defenses made him relax, tamped his heart back down his throat a little.

At the same time, the voice in his head got louder and louder. Even though the demon's be-jorted body couldn't cross the threshold, a part of it, maybe the most powerful part, was right there with them. Scot fought to ignore the voice. Kept thinking about Ethan putting that gun to his temple. The smell of gunpowder, the sight of blood mixed with fragmented brains, the screams of women who might have been actual people conscripted into demonic fantasy or just fleshy automatons conjured up out of Ethan's basest desires. He didn't want that for himself.

No matter what the voice told him, he reminded

himself in no uncertain terms, he had to ignore it. All these things did was lie.

Scot shot a glance at the back of the store. Skater Girl lay on the ground beneath the Slushpuppy machine, cradling Tanner's lifeless body in her lap, tears streaming from her eyes and sending black streaks of mascara running down her cheeks, making her look a little evil herself.

Scot wondered if the demon was in her head too. It pretty much had to be. No reason to think he was the only one hearing things, although maybe his previous experience made him more susceptible to demonic influence.

Or less?

A desperate sob drew his attention and he turned to see the clerk doubled over on top of the counter, crushing a hot dog in each hand. "I'm not even supposed to be here today," she was saying, over and over, banging her forehead against the counter. Each time she raised her head back up, a bloody blotch in the middle of her forehead grew larger and larger, blood running down her face and forming a mask just like Skater Girl's.

Hell's taint worked in mysterious ways, but Scot could tell the demon was in her, too, even though it looked like she was fighting back with all the brute force she could muster. The way she spoke, the way she moved, the peculiar glaze over her eyes. He had to get her to stop hurting herself. He approached slowly, hands out, trying not to present himself as a threat. She looked up at him and giggled, blinked blood out of her eyes, and then began sucking on one of the hot dogs, not in any sort of attempt at eroticism, more like a child sucking its own thumb for comfort. Slowly, she descended behind the counter and was quiet but for the sucking sounds.

Scot shrugged and went back to the window.

The demon was still stalking the parking lot, enraged by its own impotence in the face of a simple line of salt and snarling at the blackened sky. Although its movements were gaining fluidity as it got acclimated to the physics of Scot's world, it remained trapped on the other side of the line. The fact that this had happened at Fasmart to begin with, and they weren't fresh out of salt, was a minor miracle in and of itself. Scot's presence was another.

Over the years, he'd found his definition of the word *miracle* had gotten pretty liberal.

Of course, last time he'd been a spectator. A red-shirt who somehow hadn't ended up getting decapitated or torn in half. His friends were the ones who'd stopped it, with the exception of Ethan. Scot had just been happy to make it out alive.

Now he had to do something. This détente couldn't last.

The demon picked up the EMT's headless body and gave it a long sniff, then plunged its bearded maw into the corpse's stomach. Scot's vantage point was largely blocked by the EMT's back, so he was spared most of the gory details, except for the occasional flash of a pinkish intestine snapping in the creature's jaws, and the wet, snuffling sounds. Squelching and tearing. Cracking bones. Noises so grisly they even managed to drown out the small, whispering voice at the back of Scot's skull, however temporarily.

He recalled how the demon had started smoking

when it crossed over the salt barrier. Salt not only kept it at bay, it actually wounded the thing. He clocked the distance between the shattered windows and where the demon stood, still snacking on the EMT's innards. Fresh blood and gore stained its hockey jersey and jorts.

He looked down at the salt in his hand and figured what the hell.

Scot rushed to the open window, thumbing open the spigot on top of the salt canister, and carefully leaned out. The demon didn't notice, still preoccupied with its feast. Aiming the canister in the demon's direction as best he could, he gave it a vigorous shake.

Just as the salt left the canister, the wind kicked up again, blowing granules back in his face. Scot wiped at his eyes, feeling a grain of salt stuck under his eyelid, painfully burning him. Tears welled up and he let them come, hoping they'd wash away the pain. In the background he could still hear Skater Girl crying, and the clerk laughing to herself under the counter, muttering her mantra.

"I'm not supposed to be here today, I'm not supposed to be here today."

Scot's phone buzzed in his pocket again. He pulled it out and saw he had a voicemail from Jenny. His thumb hovered over the button to play it back. What if this was just the demon fucking with him again? He didn't think an actual call could get through. Maybe a voicemail could?

Might as well see what it's about. He clicked *play.*

"Bzzt—look, the subwoofer just got here," Jenny said, her voice faint and far-away. "I can't wait any longer, I'm going to have Jordy do it. Where the hell are you, anyway? And where's my Slushpuppy? Call me, Scot."

The EMT's body shook as the demon continued to chow down. It ripped the corpse's legs in two like a wishbone and sucked a severed limb down its gullet whole like a sword-swallower, then picked the torso back up and took a few dainty bites out of the man's stomach.

Disappointed though he was, Scot couldn't think about subwoofers or Kevin Smith right then. Not the real one, at least. The demonic parody eating an EMT in the parking lot was the only Kevin Smith he could worry about.

"You wouldn't believe me if I told you," Scot said, and hung up the phone.

The demon's face suddenly burst through the EMT's back, having chewed its way through the dead man's abdominal cavity. Jaws snapped open and closed, its long red tongue darting out to lick the air. Turning to Scot, its toothy mouth spread in a smile. It dropped the EMT's remains to the ground and slowly brought a claw to its face. A long finger with too many joints wiped away the blood around its mouth. Then its tongue slowly, sensuously licked the finger, the creature's eyes rolling back in ecstasy, its twisted body quivering with pleasure.

Scot flung the salt at it once more, but the wind just threw it back in his face. Luckily he was ready this time, and got an arm up to block the grains. The demon laughed, a horribly echoing many-voiced sound that emerged from the back of his mind as much as from the creature's blood-drenched mouth. The sound made Scot's skin crawl, made him feel dirty.

"I'm not even supposed to be here today," the clerk said in his ear.

Scot nearly jumped out of his skin. He turned to see her standing unsteadily behind him, forehead a bloody mess. Through the torn skin, he could actually see a quarter-sized bright-white hint of bone. Her breath smelled like hot dogs and rot. Though she was looking right at him, her eyes were completely vacant.

"Look, just, just go sit down over there," Scot told her, pointing back at the counter. He glanced down at the container of salt in his hand, wondering how he could douse the demon with it. Maybe he could find a fan in the back. Something to counteract the wind.

He realized the clerk was still hovering next to him.

"Welcome to Fasmart," the clerk said, dropping down to her knees right by the line of salt in front of the doors. "Our world famous Pizza Pouches are currently on sale, buy six hundred and sixty-five and get the next one free."

"What the hell are you—" Scot began, but he didn't need to finish the sentence. He knew exactly what she was doing.

The clerk darted out a hand and swept away a palmful of salt.

Breaking the protective line.

Beyond the doors, the demon howled in triumph, closing the distance to the Fasmart in two quick, ground-shaking strides. It looked down at the broken line and extended one of its three scaly arms, passing over the plane with no trouble.

Without thinking, Scot tossed salt at it. The granules landed on the beast's scaly arm and immediately starting smoking. The demon howled in pain, the arm snapping back. It shook the salt away, brought the appendage to its mouth and sucked on it, staring at Scot with black and hateful eyes.

The clerk ran her hands across the floor, wiping away salt. Scot kicked her in the shoulder, but it didn't stop her. He quickly dumped more salt on the floor to fill in the parts she'd wiped away, and tried kicking her again. No luck. He didn't want to kick her in the head. Despite what she was doing he didn't think he could bring himself to do something like that to a woman, but he didn't know what choice he had. The demon was pulling her strings now, having taken up residence in her broken mind. If he didn't find a way to stop her, she was going to let that thing in.

And then they'd all end up like the EMT.

Scot dumped more salt over the patches she'd wiped away, and then grabbed her by the ankles, dragging her across the floor. The clerk twisted in his grasp, scratching at his face. Lacquered fingernails raked his cheeks, drawing blood. Scot ignored the sting as best he could and kept hauling her away from the line of salt.

"Get offa me!" the clerk spat, grabbing a fistful of Scot's hair and yanking his head around painfully. He tried to jerk himself free and kept manhandling her towards the back of the store. Maybe he could find something to tie her up with. Did Fasmart sell rope?

The clerk kicked him, but Scot held firm. He pulled her back behind the counter, looking around for something to secure her with. Not even a string.

"Yeaghh!" the clerk screamed, kicking free of Scot's grasp. She lunged, slamming into Scot. He tottered on his legs and grabbed for the counter but fell on his ass instead.

The clerk landed on top of him, squeezing air from his lungs. Her claws slashed at his face. He put his arms up to defend himself. She raked his forearms, clawing at his skin, screaming the whole time, nonsensical, animalistic noises.

"Stop, stop," Scot pleaded, but whoever the clerk had once been could no longer hear him. The demon had her now.

Crushing fingers wrapped around his throat. He batted uselessly at her face, her hands, but he had no leverage and an ever-decreasing supply of oxygen. Nothing worked. She didn't notice his admittedly weak and ineffectual blows. Darkness crept in from the corners of his eyes.

That was a small comfort, at least. Maybe she'd kill him, or at least he'd still be passed out when those demonic jaws devoured his flesh.

The hands around his neck suddenly relaxed, Scot's mind registering a loud *thwack*. His vision began to refocus. The clerk sprawled on the ground next to him, eyes shut. Skater Girl stood over them, her board cocked back behind her shoulder, ready to deliver another blow if necessary.

"What the hell's gotten into her?" she said, her makeup and tear-streaked face slightly aquiver, but bearing a certain resolve underneath.

"The demon," Scot said, pulling himself up to his feet. "You heard that voice too, in the back of your mind?"

Skater Girl nodded. "Yeah. I told it to shut the fuck up."

"Well," Scot said, cocking a thumb at the clerk. "I think she listened."

"That's dumb."

Scot leaned heavily against the counter, taking deep breaths, every single one burning his throat exquisitely and making him glad for Skater Girl's timely intervention. Out in the parking lot, the demon simply stared at them, three arms hanging down by its sides. The whispering in the back of Scot's mind started to get louder, but there was nothing seductive about it. In fact the wordless drone reeked of desperation, like a pony-tailed club promoter on a Vegas sidewalk.

"What do we do now?" Skater Girl asked.

"Well, for one we hope *she* doesn't wake up," Scot replied. "It's bad enough having that thing out there to deal with. Other than that, salt hurts it, can even *kill* it in large enough quantities, but every time I try to throw salt on it through the window the wind kicks up again, blowing it away."

"What about holy water?" Skater Girl said, pointing to a Dasani-stocked cooler. "Maybe we could, like, bless the water or something and dump it over that fucker's ugly head?"

"Are you a priest?"

"Do I have to be?"

"Probably," Scot said. "Last time somebody tried that. It didn't end well for them."

"I'm not even going to ask. Should we, like, call somebody then? The cops or, I don't know, the army?"

Scot sighed. "Try your phone."

Skater Girl pulled out her phone and squinted at it. "It says *No Service*. And there's like a demonic-looking emoji." She punched a few buttons and held the phone up to her ear. Skater Girl nodded a few times, then her face twisted in anger and she spat out, "No, fuck *you.*" She hung up and put the phone back in her pocket.

"Guessing you didn't get through to 911?"

Skater Girl shook her head. "Those demons are seriously rude."

"They're not exactly a fan of outgoing calls."

"I guess not. Dicks." The clerk stirred at their feet, a slight moan escaping her lips. Skater Girl cracked her over the head with the board again. "Umm, are we like in hell?"

"Not exactly. More like in between. We're all trapped here together, you, me, and that ugly motherfucker out there, in between worlds, in between moments. Like a time loop. And the only way to break it is if we kill *him*—" Scot jabbed his chin at the demon, eyeing them from the parking lot, "—or he powers himself up enough to break free."

Skater Girl frowned. "How's he going to do that?"

Scot pointed at what was left of the EMT. "That's one way. Or if he turns us. You know, those whispers."

"Huh. How do you know all this?"

"Stuff I picked up. From last time." Or so he thought. Nobody'd given Scot the manual, and if such a thing existed it was probably locked in the basement of the Vatican, far away from anyone who'd actually use it.

Scot still didn't know Skater Girl's name. Part of him wanted to ask her, but part of him figured it would just make him feel worse if the demon ripped her head off and snapped her sternum in half with its jaws and slurped her soul out of the husk like the savory sweet innards of a freshly-microwaved Hawaiian-style Pizza Pouch.

Even with the line of salt protecting them, he was

starting to worry it was only a matter of time before the demon ate them, soul and body.

Unless.

"I've got an idea," Scot said. "But you're not going to like it."

"What?" Skater Girl said, raising an eyebrow.

"You saw what that thing did to the EMT, right?"

Skater girl nodded.

"Well, I'm thinking we give it something else to eat. But we use this," Scot held up the canister of salt, "to give it a little indigestion. What do you think?"

"Yeah, that sounds good or whatever, but what do you mean I won't like it?"

Scot pointed at Tanner's body, crumpled underneath the Slushpuppy machine. "*That's* what we're going to have to give it to eat."

"Uh uh, no way," Skater Girl said, vigorously shaking her head. "That's my *brother*, dude. We can't just let that thing *eat* him."

Scot grabbed her by the shoulders, looking hard into her brown eyes. "That *was* your brother," he said, a little more harshly than he meant to. "Now it's just meat."

Skater Girl pulled away from him. "You're sick, dude. I'm not doing that to Tanner. Look, why don't we just, like, give him *her?*" She pointed at the comatose clerk at their feet.

"Because she's still alive," Scot said. "What, you want to kill her? Now who's the sick one?"

Skater Girl shrugged. "She almost let that thing in. *And* she attacked you, why are you defending her?"

"Because I know how this works," Scot hissed. "That

wasn't *her* doing all that. That was the demon. You heard it whispering yourself. You know what it's trying to do, in our heads. Her problem is just that she listened."

"So?"

"So you can't blame her for that—it's hard to say no. Believe me, I know. The fact that you were able to and she wasn't says more about you as a person than her. Saying yes is practically the default. So no, I don't think she deserves to die for that. And if we can kill this thing, maybe she'll go back to normal."

"Normal?"

"As normal as things can get after something like this."

Skater Girl took a deep breath, looked at the clerk on the floor, then over at her brother. "I don't know," she finally said. "It just doesn't seem right."

Scot shot another glance at the parking lot. The demon was standing next to his truck now, looking it up and down. One of its three claws reached out and caressed the hood, leaving a shallow gouge in the paint. He wasn't sure what it was doing, but the fact that it wasn't just standing there staring at them probably wasn't good. Though they might appear dumb at first, unused to things like gravity and the other assorted rules and trappings of the physical world, in Scot's experience demonic manifestations still harbored a base, singular intellect. They weren't just slavering beasts, they were possessed of a sort of intelligence. One bent entirely on destruction, in all its myriad forms.

"If you've got another idea, I'm all ears. But think about it. What would your brother want? If he knew there was some way he could help save his sister, I think he'd—"

"Tanner was a selfish little twat," Skater Girl said. "You saw him, right before he—he wasn't doing anything. He wasn't *going* to do anything. He was just going to sit there and cry and hope that someone would come along and save us. Tanner lived his whole life like that. Always leaning on my mom for help. You know she did his homework for him? Meanwhile she wouldn't even help me with mine, the only time anyone noticed me was when I was doing something wrong, and Tanner, goddamn *Tanner,* he's just this useless sack of *nothing* and he gets to be the golden child, just because he was born like thirty-seven seconds after me—"

"Hey," Scot said, snapping his fingers. "I get it. So let's put him to work."

Out in the parking lot, the springs of his S10 creaked. The demon pushed against the truck, its unnatural strength causing the vehicle to slide a couple inches. Cocking its head in surprise at the slight sliding movement, the demon looked at its three claws, put them all up against the side of the truck, and shoved. With a loud groan the truck scooted a couple feet over into the next parking spot. Or where the next parking spot would have been, if the paint marking its bounds hadn't been superheated and transmogrified into a pentagramic drill.

"Look, we don't have much time," Scot said. "See what it's doing out there? That thing's got a plan in mind. And trust me, we really don't want to find out what it is. What's it gonna be?"

Skater Girl looked at the demon in the parking lot, now circling the truck, a malevolent and obsessive look on its bearded and scaled face as it lashed out, rocking the truck on its springs, casting a glance to the storefront and back again. Then she shot another look at what was left of Tanner. She exhaled a long breath in her dead brother's general direction.

"Okay," she said. "I guess it doesn't really matter much anyway."

"Good," Scot said, releasing his grip on the miniature baseball bat the clerk kept hidden behind the counter.

"Run over to the automotive section and see if you can find some duct tape." Scot pointed at a shelf covered in broken glass. He waited until Skater Girl had turned her back, then ducked down and went through the clerk's pockets. His fingers touched hard plastic, and he knew he'd found what he hoped would be in her pocket. A box cutter. Luckily she hadn't used it on him. Probably didn't have the presence of mind with the demon running things in her skull. It was why she'd acted like an animal, lashing out madly, clawing him. The thing in charge didn't even know what a box cutter was, it was just blindly pulling biological levers and giggling at the chaos it created.

Scot took the box cutter and a container of salt and walked over to Tanner's body. The kid's eyes were still open, staring up at the cardboard cutout of Toxie. He set his supplies down and then ran a palm across Tanner's still-warm face, forcing his eyes shut. Despite everything that was going on, he really didn't want to look into the kid's eyes when he did what he was about to do.

Out in the parking lot, the springs in his truck started to creak.

"You got that duct tape yet?" he shouted over his shoulder.

"Looking for it," Skater Girl replied. "It's supposed to be right here. Shit, maybe they're out of stock?"

Scot pulled up Tanner's black Buzzcocks t-shirt, revealing a pale chest with a handful of wiry black hairs. He appraised the kid's stomach. "Check the back of the shelves. Like, look behind everything else?"

Something clunked to the ground. Skater Girl cussed. Scot waited, box cutter in hand. What he was about to do was going to freak her the fuck out. He wasn't excited about it. In fact he wasn't entirely sure he could go through with it. But he had to try. Otherwise they were completely screwed. He didn't have a single other bright idea.

"Oh, I think I found it!" Skater Girl called back. "There was a roll stuck behind this can of oil."

"Good, hurry!" Scott yelled.

Creeeeeeeeeeeeeak.

Creak. Creak, creak, creak.

The noises from the parking lot increased in tempo. Whatever the demon was trying to figure out was nearly figured. They were almost out of time.

He sensed Skater Girl standing behind him. "Here," he said, holding out his free hand.

She placed the duct tape in it and took a step back. "What are you going to do?"

"Look, you might want to turn around."

"What?"

"I'm serious. Turn around. I dunno, maybe go grab a beer or something from the cooler. Chill out for a minute."

"Chill out? What the hell do you mean chill out? And besides, I'm fifteen, dude."

"And you've never had a beer? Definitely go grab one

then, you might be dead in the next couple minutes. You really want to die without ever having a beer?"

Skater Girl didn't reply, but he heard her walk away and the pressure seal pop when she opened the cooler. Scot kind of wished he'd asked her to grab him one, but he needed steady hands for what he was about to do.

Another *creak.* Followed by a small giggle, so quiet it was almost inaudible, and Scot wondered whether it was coming from inside or outside his own brain. Too fast the giggle grew, quickly building, multi-layered voices all *tee-heeing* together, interspersed with sickly hacking coughs, building to a crescendo of full-throated laughter. The sound reverberated in his head like a series of car crashes, one wrecked Escalade right after the other.

"Dammit," Scot cried, and plunged the box cutter into Tanner's stomach.

He had to really lean into the tiny blade to get it to do what he wanted. Grunting and sweating, he dragged the box cutter down the kid's abdomen to his belly button, sawing through layers of skin and fascia, grimacing at the blood bubbling up from the thin and jagged line. The blood slicked his fingers, and he struggled to hold on to the handle. All the while, the demon's laughter and the accompanying creaking made his pulse race.

Over by the cooler, he heard the pop and fizz of a beer being opened. *At least she's not watching,* he thought.

Scot went back to the top of the kid's ribcage and went over the cut, so much blood spilling from Tanner's torso he could barely see what he was doing. Going by feel didn't help much either, since the kid's pale stomach and his own hands were so slippery. The one saving grace was that none of this seemed real. Scot's mind couldn't even connect what he was doing to the fetal pig he'd dissected back in college, let alone to the blubbering and crying young boy who'd used his phone to film a homeless guy's seizure a lifetime ago. The thing in front of him was no more human than the laughing beast in the parking lot.

Once he'd gone over the cut a few times, he put the box cutter down and thrust his hands into the hole. Tanner's flesh was still uncomfortably warm, and the gooey heat of his abdominal cavity reminded Scot of the plastic bags of heated gel they wrapped around your hands during a manicure. He gritted his teeth and pulled, stretching the hole as wide as he could, ripping layers of subcutaneous fat apart. He just needed a space big enough to fill with salt. Enough that the demon wouldn't be able to shake it off, or spit it out.

He'd burn the fucker from the inside out.

Scot took a fistful of intestine and starting pulling it out, Tanner's pinkish guts calling to mind the burst casings of the hot dogs still rotating on the grill, so overcooked now that even the monster outside probably wouldn't touch them. Said monster was still laughing, but the sound was starting to peter out. Whatever it was planning on doing, it was going to do it soon. Scot had to hurry.

"What the hell are you doing?" Skater Girl asked, her voice a choked shriek.

"Don't fuckin' look!" Scot shouted, unspooling guts. "Just go over there and drink your damn beer."

"But you're—"

"Now!" Scot growled, not even bothering to look up from what he was doing.

Taking the box cutter, he sawed through the end of the intestine in his fist. Guts were harder to cut through than the skin had been, but he split them all the same. His nostrils filled with the tangy scent of shit, and he nearly gagged for the first time since he'd started disemboweling the dead skater boy.

Tossing the clump of guts to the side with a wet *splat,* Scot ripped the top off the salt container and dumped it into the cavity he'd created, then emptied the other container for good measure. Then he pulled the wound closed and started ripping off strips of duct tape with his teeth. All the blood made the tape not want to stick, so he pulled off his shirt and mopped it away, then awkwardly wrapped duct tape around the kid's midsection, roughly turning the body, which was lighter than he'd thought it would be.

When he was done, he leaned back on his heels and regarded his handiwork, then quickly pulled the kid's shirt back down to hide the DIY surgery. "Yo, come give me a hand," he yelled.

Skater Girl walked back over, her body shaking. "What are we going to do now?"

"Now," Scot said, "we give this thing a motherfucking tummy ache. Help me get him up."

Skater Girl swallowed hard, then a look of steely resolve came over her face. She bent down and threw an arm under her brother's armpit, then Scot did the same. Grunting, they lifted the dead skater to his feet, and started hauling him towards the front of the store.

The monster was standing directly behind Scott's

S10, looming over it, grinning at them malevolently. Scot and Skater Girl staggered to a stop and locked eyes with the demon.

"We've got a little peace offering for you," Scot said. "Hungry?" He pretended to take a bite out of Tanner's head and pantomimed chewing.

The demon cocked its head to the side, like a dog being offered a hidden fistful of Pupperoni. Its serpentine tongue slithered out of its mouth and licked its lips hungrily.

And then, most perverse of all, it nodded.

"Good, come on then."

Scot and Skater Girl hauled Tanner closer and closer to the windows, to the line of salt that was the only thing protecting them from the monster outside. "Come and get it, boy," Scot said, now feeling like he actually was talking to a dog. "Come and get it."

The demon watched them approach, but didn't move from its position behind the truck. Scot wondered why it didn't come closer. *Maybe it remembers when you threw salt at it,* Scot thought. *Twice.*

They passed the counter. The clerk lay in a heap, still not moving. The final blow Skater Girl administered had apparently done the trick. Scot hoped the woman wasn't dead.

After all, she wasn't even supposed to be there today.

Scot and Skater Girl paused at the shattered entrance to the store. "Okay," Scot said, "on three we toss him out. Just make sure the toe of his shoe doesn't break the line, alright? Keep it clean. Got it?"

Skater Girl set her jaw and nodded. "Got it. No breaking the line. No problemo."

"Good," Scot said, taking a deep breath. "On three. One. Two." He tensed his muscles, ready to toss Tanner's body through the front of the store.

"Three."

Scot and Skater Girl both grunted and threw her brother out the empty doorframe, narrowly avoiding the ring of salt, at the exact same moment the demon put its three gnarled claws on the back bumper of Scot's Chevy S10 and *pushed*.

Scot had time to scream an abbreviated "Fu—" and dive out of the way.

The truck came crashing through the entrance, tearing out what remained of the doorframe and coming to a stop half-in, half-out of the convenience store. Scot rolled into a display of Hostess snack cakes, plastic-wrapped treats softly pummeling him as they fell from their hooks. He quickly pushed himself to his feet, heart beating a mile a minute, and surveyed the damage.

A single hand of Tanner's stuck out from under the front of the truck. Their poisoned offering was trapped beneath his ride. Scot looked around for Skater Girl, didn't see her.

"You okay?" he yelled.

"Yeah," a voice called from beneath a pile of Tostitos bags. "I think I rolled my ankle, but I'm all right."

"That's good," Scot said, "real good. Look, Tanner's stuck under the truck, I'm going to try to get him out—" he stopped midsentence, stared at the two front tires of his truck. They'd broken the ring of salt.

"Shit—" he started to say, but was interrupted by a peal of hideous laughter from outside. The springs of his S10 creaked with demonic weight as it jumped on the bed, splintering Scot's beloved longboard in half. The demon dug its three clawed hands into the top of the truck, rending metal squealing at its touch, and then crawled over the cab and down the front, the edges of the hood bending upwards under its weight.

Somewhere beneath all those bags of Tostitos, Skater Girl screamed.

The demon's head snapped in her direction, nostrils flaring, tongue testing the air. Scot backpedaled, kicking snack cakes out of his way. *Salt, I need more salt,* he thought. He looked around wildly. There had been another two or three canisters of the stuff. Where was it?

He couldn't remember. And in the disarray at the front of the convenience store he despaired of actually finding it. The piles of prepackaged snacks, the warped and collapsing infrastructure of the store, the devilish giggle in the back of his head that wouldn't kindly SHUT THE FUCK UP, all of it combined to conspire against him.

The demon lunged off the hood of the S10, crashing down to the floor and snarling loudly. Skater Girl threw a bag of chips at it and ran towards the back of the store. The thing gave chase, its too-large body levelling the remaining shelves of snacks, one of its three arms clipping a jumbo thermos of coffee and knocking it over. Sludgy black Fasmart java spilled all over the floor, and the demon's taloned feet slipped in the mess, toenails scrabbling against the tile floor to find purchase.

Scot dove into a pile of Combos, tossing bags of food aside, looking for the salt. Crashing and growling sounds echoed from the back of the store. Something shattered.

"Keep it busy!" Scot yelled. "I'm looking for the salt!"

"I'm trying!" Skater Girl yelled back.

Scot sat up and looked around, wondering where the salt might be. He pushed the magazine rack back, a few copies of surfing and tattoo rags spilling out of it. He kicked the glossy periodicals out of the way. Nothing.

Something heavy smashed against the floor. He shot a look over his shoulder and saw Skater Girl disappear into the back. The demon tried to follow her, but its shoulders and torso were too wide to fit. It stuck in the doorframe, grunting and trying to push its way through.

"Shit!" He had the perfect opportunity to take the thing out. If only he could find some more salt.

Then his eyes landed on the broken line of salt around the store. Though it no longer protected them, it was still *salt*. He could use it, he just had to figure out a way to pick it up.

Scot snatched a surfing magazine off the ground, flipping it open to the subscription cards in the middle. He carefully tore along the perforated line and held the card aloft for a moment, inspecting it. Satisfied, he nodded to himself and looked around for something to scoop the salt into.

At the back of the store, the demon howled, trying to force its way through the too-small doorway. Flecks of paint chipped and fluttered to the ground. The Calgary Flames jersey caught on a stray nail, sticking out of the wall in defiance of all OSHA requirements, and ripped. Scot wondered what Skater Girl was doing in the back. Hopefully something helpful, like finding a cache of Morton's and a shotgun.

That would have been preferable. Load up both barrels with rock salt, unload them in the thing's bearded face at sixteen-hundred feet per second.

But beggars can't be choosers.

He rushed to the Slushpuppy machine and grabbed an empty souvenir cup, giving Toxie a nod as he pulled the cup free from its stack. Then he bent down to the ground and scooped salt with the subscription card. His hands shook, his pulse racing in his veins. He spilled more salt on the floor than he got in the cup. Scot wasn't sure how much he needed. He figured he'd just get as much as he could, and pray it was enough.

The beast continued to howl. Scot continued to scoop. He worked his way around the perimeter of the store, picking up the same salt he'd just laid down. More and more of the substance made it in. Pretty soon a quarter of the Slushpuppy cup was sparkling with salt crystals. He shot a look at the monster, who was still preoccupied with Skater Girl in the back. Still trying to force its way through the doorway, which was miraculously holding against the thing's ungodly bulk. Then one of the demon's claws sliced through the air and ripped into the drywall on the side of the doorframe. Dust filled the air, demonic claws tearing out chunks of the wall. The creature threw its head back and laughed as it tore the walls apart.

"What the hell are you doing out there?" Skater Girl yelled over the sounds of the beast's claws and merriment.

"Almost done," Scot said, shaking a little more salt into the cup.

"Well, hurry! It's tearing through the wall!"

He wasn't really sure how much he needed, but a third of a cup would have to be enough. He took a deep breath and hurried down the sole remaining aisle in a crouch, eyes glued to the back of the demon's torn hockey jersey. The thing was so intent on tearing down the wall that it didn't notice his approach.

He held the cup tightly in his hand, appraising the creature's corrupt body. It had stooped to be able to walk around in the store. He figured he'd dump the cup of salt directly on the thing's head. Maybe melt its brain, if he was lucky.

Passing the cash register, a hand shot out from behind the counter and grabbed Scot's ankle. The clerk's nails dug into his flesh and Scot screamed as he fell forward. He desperately held onto the cup, clamping a hand on top of the open mouth to prevent too much salt from falling out.

He landed hard on his shoulder, feeling something pop inside of him. *Gonna have a bruise tomorrow,* Scot thought, and then realized how stupid that sounded. If he didn't get away from the clerk, there wasn't going to *be* a tomorrow.

Especially since his hands were empty.

The cup of salt lay a few feet away, most of it spilled on the ground. His heart sank at the sight of their salvation scattered all over the floor.

The demon continued ripping the walls of the Fasmart apart.

Scot lashed out with his free foot, heel smashing into the clerk's head. She shrieked, but her nails bit in harder.

She yanked his body back, still far stronger than

any human had a right to be, pulling Scot under the counter, slashing at his face again, teeth snapping open and shut. Flecks of drool spattered his face. Blood dripped from the wound on her forehead, landing on his cheeks.

"Get the hell *off* me," Scot said, lashing out wildly with his arms and legs. He beat at the clerk's shoulders. She grinned and wrapped her fingers around his throat. Just like before. Her grip felt like an iron vise. Scot tried to pry her off. No dice—she was just too damn strong.

He searched the shelves below the cash register for something he could use. Found the miniature baseball bat.

Frantically gasping for air that wouldn't come, Scot grabbed the minibat off its shelf and swung it as hard as he could at the clerk's head. The bat connected with a muffled thump, her head snapping to the side. Her grip relaxed just enough for Scot to shift his weight and push her off. He quickly got to a knee and brought the bat down again, right between her eyes.

Again.

And again.

Once more with feeling.

Scot smashed her with the bat until the clerk's eyes rolled back and she toppled over. He pulled himself to his feet just in time to see the demon rip a huge hole in the wall. The ceiling started to bow in.

"Jesus, will you help me already!" Skater Girl screamed from somewhere in the back as the demon stepped through the hole.

Scot glanced at the cup of salt, most of it spilled on the floor and too far away. Without thinking, he snatched a burst hot dog off the grill and yelled, "Hey!"

The demon bent its bearded face over its shoulder to glare at him, jaws snapping angrily.

Scot threw the hot dog. The over-cooked meat sailed through the air, tumbling end over end. He'd been aiming for the creature's face, but instead it landed on a scaly trapezoid, poking out of the hockey jersey like a cold-shoulder sweater.

The demon howled in pain, its flesh emitting a small puff of smoke.

Scot stared at the wound. Looked back at the hot dogs. Back at the wound again.

Fucking sodium!

Scot grabbed another hot dog and tossed it at the creature, nailing it in the back. It howled again, spinning around to face him. Scot threw one more, hitting it on the cheek. The demon brought one of its three claws to its face, inhuman eyes afire with rage and hatred.

"Yeah! How you like that, asshole?" Scot shouted. But the hot dogs, while distracting, weren't enough to put the creature down for the count. The sodium wasn't pure. The over-cooked pork rectums holding the dogs together were also protecting the demon.

The demon growled and charged.

Scot chucked the last wiener, not bothering to look where it landed, and dove for the spilt cup of salt. He landed on the floor just out of reach and scrabbled across the tiles, fingers reaching for the rim of the cup.

Twisted black toenails clinked on the floor in front of him.

A scaly hand grabbed the back of Scot's neck, lifting him into the air, the whole room spinning around like a carnival ride.

"Shit!" he yelled, flailing his arms and legs, connecting with nothing, hanging at the end of one of the demon's three arms. The demon yelped and dropped him.

Scot hit the ground, confused as hell. The demon gaped at its own slightly-smoking palm.

He rubbed the back of his neck. His skin was still kind of sticky from his earlier dip in the ocean.

An ocean filled with salt water.

Scot popped up in the best version of a kung fu stance he could think of on short notice. "Yeah, how you like *them* apples?" He threw a couple punches in the air, hoping he looked as impressive as he thought he did, and motioned to the demon with a single finger. The demon looked at him dubiously and took a step back.

"Come on, you want a piece of me or what?" Scot's salty skin positively glowed as the Cool Water-scented essences of every New Jersey tough guy who ever existed filled his veins with their douchey power. Ronnie from *Jersey Shore*. Christopher Soprano. The Rat Pack, Jon Bon Jovi, even Jay himself, nodding approvingly and mouthing *snootch to the notch.*

He was gonna kick this demonic motherfucker's ass.

Until the demon snatched up the cash register and threw it at him.

Scot started to jump out of the way, but the register clipped him in the chest and then he was staring straight up at the lame-ass popcorn ceiling, pondering the water stains. One actually looked like Jay—maybe shaking his head sadly this time. *Smooth move, lunch box.*

So much for the glow.

Snap.

Scot wrenched his head up. The demon had slapped on a latex glove from the box behind the counter, the ones the clerk was supposed to use when handling the hot dogs but probably didn't, its talons piercing the fingertips. It flexed its claw experimentally.

"On second thought, maybe we just call it good?" Scot said.

He shrieked as the latex-gloved demon snagged a fistful of hair and pulled him closer, bringing Scot's face within inches of its own perverted visage. Blackened and cracked lips parted, forming a mirthless smile. Waves of warm and fetid air washed over him, sickening his stomach. He needed to fight. His skin was still covered in salt crystals, after all. He balled up his fists but the stench sucked the strength from his body. He could barely hold his own head up, his chin fell into his chest.

Gently, the demon placed the box of latex gloves under his jaw and brought his gaze back up to meet its own. Blazing points of white light, lost in deep pools of strangely black sclera, regarded him with an expression so foreign he could not begin to understand it.

In the back of his mind, the sweetly sibilant voice whispered anew. A litany of promises, every last one ringing false, but that hardly mattered. Scot sensed himself tuning in, even though he knew that voice was just building a pile of horseshit buzzing with flies. Images formed in his mind, 3D dioramas sculpted out of dung but the closer he looked, the more real they seemed. He saw himself in the service bays at SavMore, happily installing a subwoofer while a guy in jorts and a hockey jersey looked on approvingly, and then the jorted man rested a hand on his shoulder and a word balloon popped out of his mouth. *Say, you're pretty funny, you ever thought about acting?*

Me? Scot's word balloon replied.

That's right, Kevin Smith said, nodding, now looking like an honest-to-goodness, flesh and blood human being. *I've got this script for* Clerks 3, *but Jeff Anderson says he's too* busy, *quote unquote—I think he's doing some multi-level marketing thing. Maybe a cult, who knows. So now I'm thinking what if Dante gets a job right here at SavMore? Sounds like something I'd come up with anyway. You'd be his new sidekick. You look like the kind of guy who's got a good* Star Wars *rant or three in you, what do you say?*

What *did* he say, indeed? Scot opened his mouth, ready to say *yes, yes, a thousand times yes*—

"Hey, shithead!"

The demon cocked its head at the noise just before a cloud of white vapor engulfed them both.

Smoke billowed around them, momentarily disorienting Scot. His eyes burned. The demon screeched and dropped him to the floor. Above him the creature's obfuscated form writhed in pain, skin smoking. Scales blistered and cracked, popping like the boiling asphalt in the parking lot. The creature's three claws batted at its flesh.

Scot's fingers found the cup of salt, whatever was left in it, and he rolled away, coming to his feet. He wiped at his eyes with a forearm, staggering away from the demon and right into a cooler. He gasped for air, lungs aflame. Through a skein of tears he looked around the room and saw Skater Girl emptying the rest of the fire extinguisher in the creature's direction.

"Nice save," Scot panted, desperately trying to suck air into his lungs.

"Whatever," Skater Girl said. "We gotta finish this thing."

The creature howled horribly, its high-pitched anguish assaulting Scot's eardrums. But the cloud of vapor was dissipating. Scot could see the demon's dark outline through the white smoke, becoming ever clearer. The sodium bicarbonate had wounded it, more than the hot dogs—undoubtedly its insides were burning along with its outsides. But when the cloud dissipated, the creature would be coming for them again.

Wounded, maybe.

But also angrier.

Scot shook the salt in the bottom of the cup. A paltry amount.

Fuck it, Scot thought. *Sometimes you just gotta go for it.*

The demon clawed ineffectually at the air around it, still irritated by the vapor from the fire extinguisher. Scot charged down the aisle. The plastic Slushpuppy cup in his hand wasn't just a flimsy mile marker on the road to adult-onset diabetes, it was an instrument of holy vengeance, a flaming sword, ready to strike down evil in the name of righteousness.

Ten feet.

Sweat erupted on Scot's brow.

Five feet.

Heart pounding, he gripped the cup tighter, a primal scream building in his throat.

Three feet.

Scot leapt into the dissipating cloud of fire extinguisher spew and tossed his salt right in the demon's stupid face.

The creature recoiled, screaming in pain. Scot's momentum carried him forward and he slammed into the creature's chitinous chest, bouncing off and landing on the floor, his skin slick with something slimy from the impact.

"Graaaaaaaaaaaaaahhhhhhhhhhhhhh!" the demon roared.

A flailing claw sliced down through the air, catching Scot's bare shoulder. He screamed, the talon tearing his flesh.

He pulled away from the bladed appendage. The claw swung at him again, scoring the floor instead. Scot staggered to his feet and backed up until he ran into the counter. His fist closed tight over the stinging wound on his shoulder.

The cloud from the fire extinguisher vanished. Smoke poured from the demon's head. It howled in agony, flesh broiling. Three claws went to its face, and the thing tore its own squamous flesh open in desperation. Boiling black blood ran down its arms, more river than rivulet. Scaly skin hissed and popped and cracked and the thing sank to its knees. The inside of the Fasmart filled with a hideous stench far fouler than the demon's breath.

But much more satisfying.

"Die!" Skater Girl screamed, bashing the crumpling demon over the head with the empty fire extinguisher. The melting monstrosity flopped to the ground and continued its dissolution, putrefying flesh oozing over the tiles.

"Come on!" Scot rushed to the front of the store, the demon's wailing and the smoke pouring from its body driving him forward. He didn't want to breathe any of that shit in. He heard Skater Girl's Vans slapping across the tiles behind him, picking her way through overturned shelves of processed meats. They crawled through the front windows and collapsed in front of the store, staring at the parking lot. The asphalt wasn't boiling anymore, having dried into uneven lumps over Darla's burned body.

Scot looked up at the sky. Color and light seeped back in. He breathed a long, luxurious sigh of relief. The demon was dying, its grip on the Fasmart slipping. Soon the time loop would snap and they'd be back in the real world.

The headless, ravaged body of the male EMT still oozed blood and bile onto the concrete. They'd have a hell of a lot of explaining to do.

For a time, Scot and Skater Girl just sat there, lightly leaning against each other. Trying not to listen to the horrid screams from inside the Fasmart. The sky continued to brighten as the demon's cries decreased in volume and ferocity, until they were merely a squeak.

Then they died out altogether.

The sun flamed back into existence like a struck match in a dark closet, and a moment later the lights ringing the parking lot winked out. Scot took a deep breath, feeling the warmth on his skin, not even giving a damn about the slash on his shoulder. The world was back.

He stood up and stretched, surveying the devastation. Everything from Darla's buried body to the eviscerated EMT to his own S10 sticking half-in and half-out of the Fasmart storefront looked different in the light, simultaneously more and less real. Scot stifled a laugh. Skater Girl coughed next to him. He looked down and met her gaze and they both lost it at exactly the same time, man and girl erupting in wild peals of laughter. Tears streamed down their faces, even though they knew there wasn't anything fucking funny about what they'd just been through.

Except for everything.

"Come on," Scot said, stepping back through the shattered front window of the Fasmart. "Let's go have a look."

They crept back into the devastated store, bags of chips popping open under their feet. Neither glanced at Tanner's body, caught under the wheels of the S10, nor did they look behind the counter to see what had become of the clerk. Instead they kicked beef jerky out of their way, shoved display cases to the side. Scot led the way to the back of the store, opened the cooler, and took out two beers, handing one to Skater Girl.

"Cheers," he said, popping the top and raising his can to her. "Figured we're due a celebratory brewsky."

She clinked hers against his and nodded, and they both drank deep.

"You're like the worst influence ever," Skater Girl said through a mouthful of beer. "But holy shit, dude, we just like killed a demon. Or whatever."

Scot smiled. "You're right. We goddamn did."

They walked across the rest of the devastated store, passing Toxie's mutated and smiling face. The cardboard cutout and the Slushpuppy machine were the only things to escape the carnage. Scot paused at the machine, set his beer down for a moment, and poured a sixty-four ounce banana Slushpuppy. "For my boss," he said, holding it up.

"Banana? Eww," Skater Girl said, brushing past him, eager to see what had become of the demon.

Scot picked his beer up and followed, a cold drink in each hand. Just like a regular Joe Sixpack at the big game. Or the movies. He thought about his once-in-a-lifetime opportunity to meet Kevin Smith, to install his idol's new subwoofer, his own equanimity surprising himself. *Easy come, easy go.* He'd killed a demon, and saved a teenage girl to boot. Granted she'd also saved him. They'd saved each other, really. And that was cool. And if Scot really thought about it, Kevin Smith wasn't just the guy who'd made *Clerks, Mallrats, Chasing Amy, Dogma, Jay and Silent Bob Strike Back, Clerks 2, Cop Out, Red State,* and *Tusk.* He'd also made fucking *Zack and Miri Make a Porno,* which was a total piece of dog shit.

Not to mention *Yoga Hosers,* whatever the fuck *that* was supposed to be.

"Whoa, check it out," Skater Girl said.

The homeless guy lay in a pile of black ash, arms outstretched like he was making ash angels, the demonic flesh that formerly encased his body burned away. His face was slack, his eyes closed, his mouth slightly open, as if he were about to say something.

"Is he?" Skater Girl asked.

Scot nodded. Dead as a doornail. He felt a sudden revulsion, recalling the way he'd torn into Tanner's abdomen, and the room spun around him. For a moment, all he wanted was to sit down. Skater Girl's hand landed on his shoulder and everything swam back into focus.

"You okay?" she asked.

"What the *hell* happened in here?" someone yelled from the front of the store.

Scot turned to see a pair of cops, one black and one white, both heavily muscled and even more heavily beer-gutted standing just outside the shattered windows. Guns drawn and pointing at Scot and Skater Girl.

Scot put on the friendliest expression he could manage and pointed at the homeless guy, dead in his pile of ash.

"He did it."

Scot Kring stepped out of his Uber, reaching back through the window to fist-bump his driver Vallabh, who'd gotten him from the remains of the Fasmart to SavMore Electronics in record time, and even hooked him up with a new shirt to boot (a too-small and slightly sweaty Padres jersey the previous passenger left in the back).

"Thanks, man."

"Any time," Vallabh said. "Just remember to give me five stars, the last guy—"

"All right then," Scott replied and made for the double doors. His shoulder ached, and the sixty-four ounce banana Slushpuppy in his hand had liquefied, but he didn't care. He'd made it. The cops bought his story, logged him as an innocent (and slightly wounded) bystander, and let him go with a shoulder full of liquid stitches.

Even though the bay doors on the far side of the store were shut, he couldn't imagine there was still an Escalade inside. The thought of Jordy getting to install Kevin Smith's system pissed him off, but at the same time *Jordy* hadn't fought a demon straight out of the pits of hell and lived to tell about it.

For the second time.

The automatic doors parted at his approach and he stepped into the cool, sterile confines of SavMore Electronics.

Oddly, Evelyn wasn't by the front door, marking off receipts with a Highlighter to ensure nobody tried to pull a fast one. In fact the front of the store was empty except for the high school kid standing behind the only open register and playing with his phone. Scot scanned the store, seeing a few shoppers browsing the cell phone section, before finally noting the wall of yellow polo shirts keeping a crowd back from the TV department.

"What the—"

"Thank God you're here," Jenny said, rushing up behind him.

"Jenny, what's—"

"I've been dying for one of these bad boys," Jenny said, snatching her Slushpuppy from him and taking a lengthy slurp from the neon pink novelty straw. "Ugh, that tastes like ball sweat." Her freckled face crinkled unpleasantly. "Where the hell were you? I tried to stall for time, but eventually I had to just let Jordy do it."

Scot shot a glance over at the TV department. "Wait, what's going on over there?

"Oh, Ben Affleck came in a little while ago, he keeps trying to shove *Daredevil* Blu-Rays into the demo units."

"Gross."

"I know. I mean, I could understand if it was *Phantoms*. Anyway, this is totally warm," Jenny said, shoving the Slushpuppy back into Scot's hands. "Can you go get me another one?"

"Another one?"

"Do you really expect me to drink a warm Slushpuppy? Come on, there's a Fasmart like two blocks away."

Scot didn't want to step foot in a Fasmart just yet, and maybe ever again. "Why don't you go?"

"I'm manager-on-duty, I can't leave until they corral *Reindeer Games* over there."

Scot sighed. "Fine. I'll be right back."

Which is how Scot found himself at another Fasmart, the one down the street from SavMore that he never went to because the gas prices were always way too high and the rack of absurdly dated porno mags behind the counter made him feel old. He scoped the parking lot for homeless guys and jort-wearing demons before he walked inside, but the coast was clear. No one else was in the store. He filled up another banana Slushpuppy (this machine lorded over by a promotional poster for Warren Beatty's *Dick Tracy,* an even more outdated reference than the Toxie cartoon at the one on Garnet), completed his transaction with a much more alert clerk who didn't try to force an unwanted receipt into his hand and wasn't unduly captivated by the hot dogs on the grill and stepped back outside, wondering why the hell every trip to the Fasmart couldn't be that simple.

He froze when a black Escalade drove into the parking lot and pulled up to the pumps.

The windows were down, and he would have recognized the profile of the driver immediately even if he hadn't been bumping "Jungle Love" through his new subwoofer, freshly installed by that son of a bitch Jordy.

The hockey jersey.

The beard.

The backwards baseball cap.

Scot stood there, Slushpuppy in hand, every last bass note hitting him like a punch to the gut. Like the universe wanted to shove it in his face. *Check it out bitch, we kicked the ladder out from under you and now we're going to rub it in.*

He could have gone over to the Escalade, said hello, but he figured he'd just make an ass out of himself and then Kevin Smith would tweet about the awkward fanboy who harassed him at the gas station.

Turning to go before this particular Slushpuppy melted or he did something he'd regret for the rest of his life, Scot's shoulders slumped, and for the briefest of moments he wondered what might have happened if he'd said *yes* to all the bullshit the demon cloaked in the skin of his hero put on offer—maybe Jordy would have OD'ed on Whip-Its or something. And then Kevin Smith would have asked him to be in *Clerks 3* and everything would be awesome.

The sweet, dulcet tones of Morris Day and the Time suddenly cut out.

"Shit, I just got this installed!" the man himself griped from the pilot seat of his Escalade.

Fucking Jordy! Scot thought, and then a smile spread on his face.

"Excuse me, Mr. Smith?" he called, tossing Jenny's Slushpuppy over his shoulder where it splatted on the concrete behind him. "Mind if I take a look at that?"

Bella sat alone in her room, the last rays of fading sunlight shining weakly through her blinds, staring at walls covered in posters of people doing kick-flips and bands that favored demonic imagery. She'd always liked dark shit, but maybe not anymore. Now the skulls and horns hit a little too close to home and she kept thinking maybe she should tear down all her posters and burn them in the back yard.

The cops had grilled her and Old Guy (that was how she thought of him, since he'd never mentioned his name and she hadn't cared enough to ask), together at first until a pair of detectives showed up on-scene. Bella didn't know what to tell them, but it kind of didn't matter. Nothing could explain Darla being buried under the asphalt or the condition of her partner's corpse. Or Tanner, cut open and stuffed with salt and duct-taped back together. She admitted to being in the Fasmart, but claimed she got conked on the head early on and didn't remember a thing. Old Guy spun a similar yarn, but since it was his Chevy parked half-in and half-out of the Fasmart, that story seemed a little suspect to the five-o. He'd gotten breathalyzed, scoring a .03 thanks to the celebratory beer from the cooler. Despite this, the cops nodded along and glared at them over their mirrored shades and eventually let them go with an admonition not to leave town. Bella figured they'd make something up for the news vans lurking around the perimeter. She wasn't too concerned about getting in trouble. This kind of thing was so weird the authorities were sure to say fuck it and sweep it under the rug.

Her mother had been inconsolable, the loss of Tanner hitting her like a bag of hammers whereas for Bella it had already dulled to an ache. Various neighbors stopped by and sat with them for a while, bringing tinfoil-covered dishes nobody touched, until Bella sent them off. Then she crushed up some Xanax and slipped it into her mother's wine to get her to shut the fuck up. After all, her mother only had simple, everyday grief to contend with.

Bella had much, much more.

She rolled onto her stomach and pulled out her phone, mind abuzz with emotions. Bella still hadn't wrapped her head around the fact that her annoying brother was *gone*. In fact she kept catching herself leaning an ear against the wall her room shared with his, listening for the comforting sounds of Tanner jacking off to internet porn.

But she heard nothing.

Bella scrolled through her phone until she found the video. With everything that had happened, she'd forgotten to upload it to her various social media accounts. With a few button clicks, she rectified that situation. It *was* a pretty wild video.

Within a few minutes it garnered a couple dozen likes and even a few shares. Bella clicked refresh a few more times, dopamine juicing her brain with every new hit.

She figured what the hell, might as well watch it again.

Bella clicked play. The homeless guy went through his contortions. She winced at how shaky the video turned out—ratchet AF. The volume was still off so she thumbed the switch on the side of her phone up.

"Homina gomina glomina gliddy gloo!"

"Huh," she said, feeling a slight pang of sadness when Tanner's elbow entered the frame.

"Nibby moo moo skukka rukka hey!"

"Nibbimum scurlous influp diggium dee ibis!"

"Shut up!"

"Nimibuum storklos ferby dicktum!"

"Shut up, shut up, shut up!"

"Hey, what are you doing?"

"*Nimirum circulos inferni dicam de imis tenebris!*"

The air around her shifted slightly; first a few degrees cooler, then much, much warmer. If she'd been looking outside she would have seen a cloud passing in front of the setting sun, the sky turning black. Not the black of night, but a deeper, darker black. A color of less than nothing. Anti-nothing.

Beneath her feet, the ground began to shake.

ABOUT THE AUTHOR

Hailing from San Diego, California, Brian Asman writes horror and other weird stuff, often with a barrel-aged beer in hand and his Staffordshire terrier, Emma, at his feet. His recent credits include short stories in California Screamin', Behind the Mask: Tales from the Id, Deciduous Tales, and the upcoming anthologies Lost Films and A Sharp Stick in the Eye. He is currently the president of the San Diego chapter of the Horror Writers Association and an MFA student at UCR-Palm Desert.

ACKNOWLEDGMENTS

There are a few people without whom this novella would probably never have seen the light of day. Thanks to my mother, for all the bedtime stories. Stephen Graham Jones, for helping me whip this thing into shape and exorcising the *as*-demons. John Skipp, for writing advice and motivation in equal parts. All my critique partners, for finding the cracks in this narrative and others—Sarah Liddle, Shelly Lyons, the Circle of Darkness crew, and my friends from UCR-Palm Desert. The San Diego Chapter of the Horror Writers Association. Rose and everyone at Eraserhead for taking a chance on this weird ass story.

Thanks also to all the family and friends who've supported me over the years, who've indulged me as I've blathered on over drinks about some work in progress, beta read one of my drafts, or even published my stuff. This list is frightfully incomplete but special thanks to Jaclyn, Erik, Eric, John, Mike, Destiny, Jason, Bree, Max and Lori, Matthew and Tara, Bob and Michael at *This is Horror* and everybody else from the Story-a-Week Challenge, and so many more. This is all your fault.

And finally a few creative thank yous--Bruce Novotny for writing *Tales from an Endless Summer,* the greatest Jersey novel of all time; Jim Mahfood for being a badass artist; and of course Kevin Smith. If you ever read this book, it is my sincere and fervent hope that you won't take out a restraining order against me.

CPSIA information can be obtained
at www.ICGtesting.com
Printed in the USA
FSHW012156160219